Contents

ANNUAL 2002

Pedigree®

Published by Pedigree Books Limited
The Old Rectory, Matford Lane, Exeter EX2 4PS
E-mail books@pedigreebooks.co.uk
Published in 2001

£5.99

This is the home of
a puppy called Blue.

Let's see if she's in.

6

Knock, knock!
Open the door!

There she is.
Hello, Blue!

Here we are in Blue's living room.

Blue is sitting in the Thinking Chair. She is holding the Super Duper Notebook in her mouth.

Do you think she wants to play Blue's Clues?

8

We need a crayon
if we want to play
Blue's Clues.
Can you see one? Yes

Look at the towers
Blue has built with her
building blocks.
Can you point to the
square bricks? Yes
Which bricks are
shaped like triangles?
Which is the tallest tower?
that one
Now we're ready to play
Blue's Clues.

Look for the things with
a blue pawprint on them.

They're whose clues?
Blues clues
They're Blue's Clues!

Do you see a clue yet? No? Then let's play a game with
Felt Friends first!

Look at these two pictures of a Felt Friend. They both look the same,
but the bottom one is different. Can you say why?

What is this Felt Friend doing? Is he eating something nice? What is your favourite food?

Draw a picture of a Felt Friend eating your favourite food.

Let's follow Blue into the kitchen to see if we can see any clues there. Say hello to Mr. Salt, Mrs. Pepper and Paprika!

There are three fruits on the table. Can you say what they all are? Which one is yellow? What colour are the others?

the banana

A CLUE! A CLUE!

Do you see a clue with Blue's pawprint on it?

That's right, it's the cloth!

Let's draw the cloth in the Super Duper Notebook. Do you think Blue is trying to tell us she would like to play with it? Let's see if we can find any more clues in the kitchen.

Blue has opened the fridge. She does look hungry, doesn't she? It must be nearly lunchtime.

A CLUE! A CLUE!

Do you see the second clue?

That's right, it's the sandwich!

Let's draw the sandwich in our Super Duper Notebook. Do you think Blue wants a sandwich for lunch?

Look for the third clue on the next page to find out.

Can you see what the weather is like through the window? Perhaps Blue would like to go in the garden if it's nice.

A CLUE! A CLUE!

Blue is really happy that we have found the last clue.

It's a picnic basket!

If we draw the picnic basket in the Super Duper Notebook, we have all three clues. Now we need to go to the Thinking Chair to find out what Blue wants to do!

The Thinking Chair is the best place to be when we're thinking about Blue's Clues.

What could Blue want to do at lunchtime with a cloth, a sandwich and a picnic basket? Turn the page to find out!

The clues mean that Blue would like a picnic lunch!

She showed us the picnic cloth first. We need to put that on the grass, then we can put the picnic food on it.

Then she showed us a sandwich. Sandwiches are the best food to take on a picnic, because you can eat them with your fingers!

Finally, she showed us the picnic basket. That's what we need to carry our picnic food in!

We just worked out Blue's Clues, because we're really bright!

Come on then, Blue. Let's have a picnic lunch in the garden!

Tasty Treats

Before we go into the garden, let's get some yummy cakes for the picnic. Look at all the cakes below. Use a pencil to join up the matching pairs with a line, then say which cake is the odd one out.

Blue's Picnic Lunch

It is a warm, sunny day. Blue is going to have a picnic lunch in the garden.

She runs out of the house and looks for a nice patch of grass to sit on.

Blue finds the perfect place for a picnic. She is really looking forward to it! She sits on her picnic cloth and puts a napkin round her neck. She looks around, puzzled.

Where has her basket of food gone?

Blue has a look round the garden for her lunch. Do you see where it is? It's on Bucket and Spade's trolley!

Bring that back, Bucket and Spade! Blue will share her food with you, if you ask her nicely!

Now everyone is ready to join in the picnic.

If Blue, Bucket and Spade eat their sandwiches, they can have a delicious cake afterwards. They all love picnic lunches!

Blue has finished
her lunch now.
She is having a run
around with her
ball before she goes
back inside. There is a
snail watching her.
Can you spot it? Look at the apple tree.
Which fruit does not belong there?

This is Blue's vegetable patch.

How many tomatoes do you see? 5

How many carrots are there? 6

Can you see what Blue has been using to water the vegetables?

What is it called?

B is for Blue

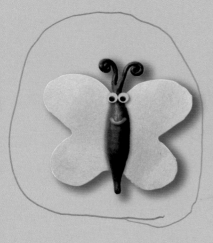

B is for Blue! Look at this picture of Blue in the garden with her friends and see if you can find ten other things beginning with the letter 'b'. The answers are at the bottom of the next page.

There are 5 caterpillars altogether in the picture.
See if you can find them all!

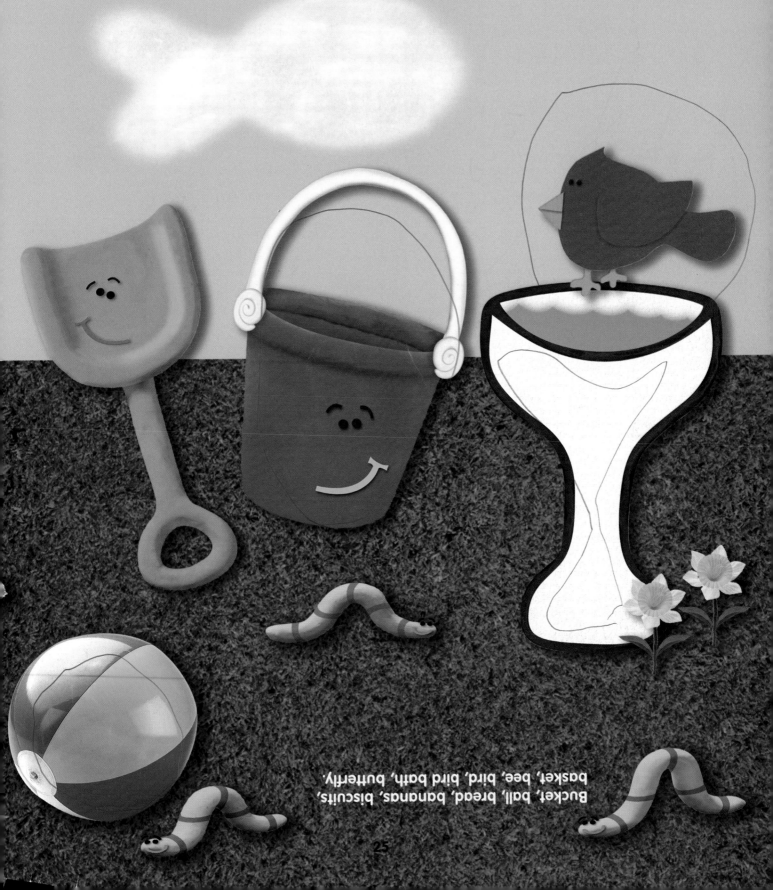

Bucket, ball, bread, bananas, biscuits,
basket, bee, bird, bird bath, butterfly.

25

Food Fun

Mr. Salt and Mrs. Pepper are making patterns with food on the kitchen table. Look at the rows of food and say what you think comes next in each one. The answers are at the bottom of the page.

pear, doughnut, orange.

26

A Funny Shopping List

Blue has come in from the garden and is looking at the shopping list Kevin has just put up on the fridge. It looks like he's got his letters all mixed up!

Unjumble the letters to help Blue see what is on the list.

The answers are at the bottom of the page.

gseg
3 4 1 2

cijue
4 3 1 2 5

noonis
2 1 4 5 3 6

pleaps
3 4 5 1 2 6

dreba
5 2 3 1 4

27

Post is Here!

Blue has come back to the living room. She knows that Post Box has a letter for her.

POST IS HERE,

POST IS HERE,

Letters come from far and near,
All year long they make me
want to cheer!

"I think it might be a party invitation, Blue,"
says Post Box.

Turn the page to see if he is right!

A Letter! A Letter!

We've just got a letter,
We've just got a letter,
We've just got a letter,
Wonder who it's from!

It's from Bucket and Spade.
They have invited Blue to their birthday party!

Blue is going to skidoo into Bucket and Spade's party.

Blue skidooed, so can you!

Turn the page to join in the fun!

Party Time

Bucket and Spade are having lots of fun at their party.

They love their little balloon dog!

There are ten other balloons in the picture. Can you find them all?

There are 5 balloons together in one bunch.

Can you see any more groups of 5?

A Message For Bucket and Spade

Blue has a special message for Bucket and Spade. Unjumble the letters below to see what it is. The answer is at the bottom of the page.

Party Bags

Blue is looking forward to getting her party bag and Bucket and Spade would like one, too. Draw a line from each toy to one of the party bags so that each bag has three different toys in it.

Bathroom Clues

Blue has trotted into the bathroom now.
Say hello to Slippery Soap!

Let's play Blue's Clues to
see what Blue wants to do.

Look for the three things
with a blue pawprint on them.

A CLUE! A CLUE!

Do you see a clue with
Blue's pawprint on it?
That's right, it's the
bubble!

Let's draw some
bubbles in the Super
Duper Notebook.
Do you think Blue is
trying to tell
us she
would like
to blow
bubbles?

36

Let's see if we can find any more clues in the bathroom.

How many toothbrushes can you see in the bathroom? Whose do you think they are? What else do you see next to the toothbrushes? What would you use it for?

Do you see the second clue? That's right, it's the towel!

A CLUE! A CLUE!

Let's draw the towel in our notebook. What do you think Blue would need a towel for? Look for the third clue on the next page to find out.

Can you see Blue's bath toys? Yes
What are they? duck
boat and a fish
What toys do you play with
in the bath? a crab and
a boat and a fish

A CLUE! A CLUE!

Well done! You've found the
last clue. It's Slippery Soap!

If we draw a bar of soap in the Super Duper
Notebook, we have all three clues. Now we
need to go to the Thinking Chair to find out
what Blue wants to do!

The Thinking Chair always helps us to solve Blue's Clues.

What could Blue want to do with some bubbles, a towel and a bar of soap? Turn the page to find out!

The clues mean that Blue wants to have a bath!

Blue showed us the bubbles first - they make bath time lots of fun! Then she showed us the towel. She needs that to get dry afterwards. Finally, she showed us Slippery Soap. She will use soap to get nice and clean!

We just worked out Blue's Clues, because we're really bright!

Blue's Song Time

You're getting good at playing Blue's Clues now! The clues show what Blue likes doing in the bath and the piano keys mean she likes to sing!

See if you can work out from the rest of the clues what two of her favourite songs are called. The answers are at the bottom of the page.

Bath Time For Blue

Blue loves bath time! Use a pencil to draw a line through the maze of bubbles and show Blue the way to her bath.

Blue's Bath Toys

As well as lots of bubbles in the bath, Blue likes to have plenty of toys to play with. Look at the shadows of her favourite bath toys below and say what you think they all are. The answers are at the bottom of the page.

a) fish b) duck c) boat d) seahorse e) starfish

43

All Clean!

Blue has had her bath now. There are still some bubbles floating around the bathroom, though.

How many can you count?

Where is Blue going now?

She is going to skidoo into the beach picture that is on the bathroom wall.

Blue skidooed, so can you!

Turn the page to join in the seaside fun!

Blue Finds A Starfish

Blue is having fun with her ball on the beach. She sees a star shape on the sand and stops to have a look at it. She wonders what it could be.

Blue looks up. Could the star have fallen down from the sky? She crouches down to take a closer look at it.

Along comes a crab. He chuckles when he sees how puzzled Blue is. "That's a starfish," he explains. "It lives in the sea. It must have got lost!"

Blue helps the starfish back into the sea by pushing it along with her nose. "Well done, Blue!" smiles the crab. Goodbye, little starfish!

Blue At The Beach

Sun, sea and sand are three things beginning with 's' that we need for a good day at the seaside! Look at this picture of Blue and her friends having fun on the beach and see if you can spot ten other things that begin with the letter 's'.

The answers are at the bottom of the next page.

There are 10 shells altogether in the picture.

See if you can find them all!

Spade, snorkel, sky, shells, swimming ring, starfish, seahorse, sunglasses, sandwich, strawberries.

Bedroom Clues

Blue has skidooed back from the beach. Where is she now? That's right, she's in her bedroom. Say hello to Tickety Tock the clock! Let's play our last game of Blue's Clues to see what Blue wants to do now.

Look for the three things with a blue pawprint on them.

They're whose clues? They're Blue's Clues!

Look for the third clue on the next page to find out.

Let's draw the quilt in our Super Duper Notebook.

Do you think Blue is trying to tell us she would like to sit on it? No

Blue's bedroom is nice and tidy. She has put her toys in the bottom of her wardrobe.

How many of the toys are animals?

What are they all called? Can you spot another animal hiding in the picture?

A CLUE! A CLUE!

Do you see the second clue?

That's right, it's the pillow!

Let's draw the pillow in our Super Duper Notebook. Look for the third clue on the next page.

53

Blue needs to put away her crayons now.
How many can you find altogether?

A CLUE! A CLUE!

Well done! You've found the last clue - a storybook for Blue!

If we draw a book in our Super
Duper Notebook, we have all three
clues. Now we need to go to the Thinking Chair
to find out what Blue wants to do!

The Thinking Chair is the best place to be when we are working out Blue's Clues. What could Blue want to do with a quilt, a pillow and a book? Turn the page to find out!

The clues mean that Blue wants to go to bed!

Blue showed us her quilt first - she snuggles up under it to keep warm! Then she showed us her pillow. It's nice and soft for her to rest her head on. Finally, she showed us a book. She wants to hear a bedtime story before she goes to sleep!

We just worked out Blue's Clues, because we're really bright!

Arty Blue

Blue loves doing pictures on the easel in her bedroom. She wants to let you have a turn now! Use your crayons or paints to draw a picture on the easel. You could draw Blue if you like!

57

Tidy Up Time!

Blue's bedroom isn't always tidy. Look at these four sleepsuits lying around on the floor! They all look the same, but one is different.

Say which one is different and why, before Blues puts them all away.

Blue's Shoes

Blue's shoes are all jumbled up! Help her to join up the pairs by drawing a line from each shoe to its partner.

Bedtime For Blue

Blue is very tired after her busy day. She is going to get ready for bed now. Look at the things below and say which things Blue needs for bedtime. Then say when she would use the other things.

Blue is going to bed now. She has enjoyed playing Blue's Clues with us!

Let's leave her to listen to her bedtime story.

Goodnight, Blue!